T0365375

THE EARTH KEEPER'S GIFT

TARA LANGELLA AND MARIA LANGELLA SORGIE

Archway Publishing books may be ordered through booksellers or by contacting:

Archway Publishing
1663 Liberty Drive
Bloomington, IN 47403
www.archwaypublishing.com
1 (888) 242-5904

ISBN: 978-1-4808-7026-0 (sc)
ISBN: 978-1-4808-7027-7 (hc)
ISBN: 978-1-4808-7025-3 (e)

Print information available on the last page.

Archway Publishing rev. date: 01/07/2019

FOREWORD

by
Frank Langella

Dear Children of All Ages,

You never quite know, do you, how the little ones are going to turn out. In this case, I am speaking of my nieces, Maria and Tara, the authors of this beautiful book. Two young women who have, from childhood, always had a special way with animals and been close to the wonders and glories of nature's gifts.

And their all grown up knowledge lets us in on the secret that those glories are not to be found where many of us may have been looking. Not to be found with eyes cast low onto our computer keys or in the apps in our cell phones.

But there, if you allow yourself to feel your place among them, in the plants and flowers and animals existing along with us. And to hopefully embrace the equally diverse human beings sharing this planet.

Nimue, our heroine, is on a journey in an effort never again to feel unseen, unheard or unloved. A place where she can dream again, hope again.

And she learns the answers are to be found in the place she is most afraid to look.

Maria and Tara have written a simple but profound message. That we are all afraid of what we don't know or understand. That we live on guard against feeling. That the real enemy is within our own hearts. And that if we can overwhelm our fears and come to understand each of us is not merely living on this planet, but an integral piece of it, we can find not only a harmony within ourselves but perhaps take steps together toward sharing the joy of The EarthKeeper's Gift

Turns out my nieces have turned out rather well. As you will learn when you turn the page.

FL

THE EARTH KEEPER'S GIFT

CHAPTER 1
NIMUE

Nimue loved riding her painted pony Cloud. She knew she only had an hour before the school bus arrived so she saddled up quickly and headed out for the trails. Cloud picked up his step as they entered the wood. He loved adventure. "Easy boy," spoke Nimue softly as she sat up in the saddle. "I know, I'm excited too." She patted the pony softly on his neck.

Nimue had a special way with animals. The pony settled at her soft touch. As they rode on, Nimue did not stop talking, to the pony, to the birds, to the trees, and all living things. An only child, who walked with a limp, this was her world. Riding her pony made her feel strong. The real world was not kind to her. Children teased her because she talked to animals and trees and walked different from them. Her parents scolded her for believing in magic and what they termed a fantasy world.

Nimue didn't believe in these people. She followed the world that was kind to her. She knew in her heart where she belonged. She giggled aloud as she sent her pony into a gallop. Nimue loved galloping through the woods. As Cloud and her turned around the bend in the trail, the pony stumbled. Nimue flew off his back and struck her head on a large rock. The pony stopped and pushed Nimue lightly with his nose. "Are you ok Nimue?" Nimue stirred and rubbed her head. "Yes, Cloud, I am fine, but my head still hurts." Nimue slowly tried to stand, but quickly fell back down.

CHAPTER 2
GRANDFATHER GINSENG

Suddenly she felt something. A magical presence. It was very old and sad. On the forest floor was a plant that she had seen somewhere before. She was drawn to its powerful spirit and awed at the same time. Something was wrong. The little plant didn't look right.

Laying her fingertips gently on its leaves she knelt down to sit beside the old wise plant. Perhaps he would like a gift, she thought. She took the moonstone she wore from around her neck and offered it to the plant. "Thank you child. The moon is beautiful like your spirit." The little ginseng shrugged and tears fell from his little ginseng face. "Everything has its season, time passes, and there is a rhythm to all things. Spring, Summer, Fall and Winter. Soon it will be only winter for my kind. For thousands of years we have cared for the earth and her creatures. We have taught humans how to grow through dreams. We are the Peacekeepers." Nimue asked, "What does the Peacekeeper do?" "I help things grow," answered Ginseng. "What kinds of things?" "All things," "Human beings?" "Yes, especially humans. Your spirits need extra looking after. That is our job to help grow your spirits. But now no one listens to the forest voices anymore."

"I know who you are Grandfather Ginseng! I remember a song you taught me once long ago. In my dreams. Follow the spirits of the plants. Open your spirit to the Living Earth. Shine forth the magic that is within you…" Grandfather Ginseng smiled and began to sing in the most beautiful language Nimue had ever heard. She wanted to learn more about the plants and their world but more than that she wanted to protect this world forever. "No Grandfather it is not too late. I have heard your song. Perhaps I can teach it to others. Other children will sing your songs and come to heal the forest. Tell me what I must do."

"Life is not an easy path child. Many humans have lost their spirits. In order to find them you must go to where the forest is deepest. There you must seek out The Earth Keeper. You must travel to the Black Woods and listen to the trees for they are the elders. Pay attention to them. They will teach you to heal the hate in man's heart. Get on your pony, he knows the way." Nimue mounted Cloud. "I am scared Grandfather Ginseng," sobbed Nimue. "It is fear that cripples you. So child, listen as I know you can and believe in what you hear, you will be protected, now go, go now," Grandfather Ginseng sternly replied. Nimue gently told Cloud to show her the way.

CHAPTER 3
BLACK WALNUT

Nimue wandered for days searching for The Black Woods. She started to get scared. She was in the middle of a whole new world and she was completely lost. The more she rode the more she started to doubt. She soon found herself surrounded by a dense pack of trees. The Black Walnuts. They would show her the way. She approached the trees and offered them her beaded bracelet. She waited for their advice. But no voice was heard. She gave them some of her crystals from her pouch and waited. No matter how hard she tried the Black Walnuts would not speak to her. She stopped to get a drink of water and saw her reflection. She began to weep. Maybe Grandfather Ginseng was playing a trick on her. Perhaps, she was crazy like everyone in the village said she was. She looked at her reflection in the water and cried. Why was she so ugly? She buried her face in her hands and wept. A crow flew overhead and landed upon one of the ugly gnarled branches. She looked again to the Black Walnuts and cried out to them. "Oh please help me, I feel so lost." She wept until her tears fell upon the tree bark.

"Well…all you had to do was ask. We cannot help your kind unless you ask us," said the Black Walnut. Nimue replied, "But I have given you one of my special crystals." The Black Walnut softly spoke, "yes…the crystals are very pretty but that is not the kind of gift we need." Nimue questioned, "I am not sure I understand Black Walnut." Black Walnut responded, "Tell me Nimue what is sacred?" Nimue hesitated and Black Walnut asked, "Is the crow sacred?" "Oh, yes," replied Nimue. "AH and the plants?" asked Black Walnut." "Yes," answered Nimue. "Me?" asked Black Walnut. Nimue nodded her head. "What about you? Are you sacred Nimue," said Black Walnut. Nimue answered softly, "yes." Black Walnut responded to Nimue firmly, "then why do you weep at your reflection?" Nimue answered again softly, "I don't know." Black Walnut explained, "How can you pay attention to the world around you when you don't look at the world inside of you. You have so much love that you are willing to give to our world and yet you don't give any to yourself. Come closer. Good. Now come place your hands upon my bark and listen with all of your being."

Nimue did as The Black Walnut instructed her. She listened with all of herself. She could hear other trees speaking to her in far off whispers and she could feel the yearning for moisture and nourishment. She was inside the tree. More than that she was the tree. And she was Nimue too. It was hard to tell where the black walnut ended and she began. She felt young and old at the same time. Images and patterns danced before her eyes. It was so beautiful inside. She wanted to stay forever. Then everything went black.

Black Walnut spoke, "I have shared my medicine with you and you have left part of your medicine with me." Nimue asked, "What is medicine and how do I use it?" "Stay with us and then perhaps I will tell you," answered Black Walnut. Nimue shouted, "But I can't do that. I can't leave my village." Black Walnut responded, "How can you learn of this place if you don't stay long enough to know it. Besides you need to strengthen your sense of self before you enter The Black Woods and that means walking away from everything you have ever known." Nimue cried, "I can't leave my village. I hate it…but somehow. I can't leave it." Black Walnut said softly, "You must travel between the worlds. In order to share medicine you cannot live in one place." Nimue continued to cry, "What if I am not strong enough?" "I know you Nimue. I know everything about you. You are strong. Remember, part of your spirit is within me. What did you see inside this old bark child?" asked Black Walnut. Nimue replied, "Beauty." Black Walnut answered back, "You saw pieces of yourself." Nimue glanced at the ground and whispered back, "No, I am not beautiful." Sternly Black Walnut responded, "That is what you believe and that is what cripples you. It is time for you to meet Rose. She will open your mind, body and spirit to love. Nimue climbed up on Cloud and the pony took her to the next place.

CHAPTER 4
ROSE

Nimue and Cloud journeyed for days and soon found themselves in the most beautiful part of the forest. A voice echoed, "Hello little one." Nimue looked up and saw a beautiful Witch Hazel Tree. She asked, "Witch Hazel, can you help me find Rose?" Witch Hazel answered, "She is right behind you Nimue." Nimue turned and looked at Rose. Nimue exclaimed, "You are so pretty." Rose giggled and replied, "Yes I know. I am awfully cute." Another plant chimed in, "Hey Rose, you are looking especially pretty today. Did you do something with your buds?" It was Horsetail. Rose answered bluntly, "No you tiny little pine tree. I haven't done a thing. Same old Rose you know. Anyway what can I do for you, Nimue?" Nimue answered," sorry but…well.ummmmm." Horsetail snapped at Nimue, "What are you doing here. Rose make her go away." Rose giggled and said, "It's his birthday Nimue and he is depressed so he doesn't wish to talk to you. Come now Horsetail you know you don't mean it tell Nimue how old you are today."

Horsetail replied, "I have been on this earth longer than animals and humans. My ancestors lived over 300 million years ago before the age of the dinosaurs. Rose doesn't understand. I have seen things. I have observed man through the ages. It is different now. The earth and people. Humans are so unkind. They are changing. There is no hope for us." Rose interrupted, "That is where you are wrong Horsetail. I understand more than you know. But we cannot close ourselves off to humans. We must help them open their hearts. Are you forgetting why we are here?" Rose then turned to Nimue, "Nimue come here. Do you know how you found yourself in this world." Nimue nodded and said, "I had an accident." Rose explained, "Nimue it was no accident. We called and you heard. Even Horsetail called you." Horsetail shouted, "I did no such thing." Nimue asked, "Why did you call me?" Rose answered softly, "We call to those who will listen. Those who have magic." Nimue smiled she knew she had magic. She felt it in her heart.

Nimue than said, "You make me happy Rose. My spirit feels lighter." Rose smiled and said, "That is part of my medicine." Nimue answered back, "Your thorns are part of your medicine too. They help protect you." Rose seemed to smile as she replied, "there's hope for you yet child."

Nimue looked over at Horsetail who was still very upset. She walked over to him and offered him one of her many beads from her pouch. She then said to him, "Horsetail you are correct. I have seen the hardness in people's hearts. I know what it is like not to be heard. What would you like me to do? What can I do for you?" Horsetail looked up at Nimue and said, "No one has ever asked before." Nimue closed her eyes, touched him gently and listened with her heart. She felt strength and power emanating from his spirit. In her mind she heard his song and felt her legs straighten out from under her. Her body felt stronger. And in her mind flowed these words, honoring our ancestors, our history and recognizing truth. Horsetail responded, "Yes Nimue. I want people to see the truth, to remember a time and place where we spoke a language, where our stories were heard, our songs sung, our spirits free." Nimue knew she would do whatever it took to give a voice to this magical place.

Just then Willow spoke out, "I have medicine too." Nimue placed her hands upon the bark of willow and the images flooded through her mind. Flexibility and regeneration. The ability to flow with change. Rose spoke, "Ok Nimue look at Witch Hazel over there. What do you believe is her medicine?" Nimue answered confidently, "Her bark helps with cuts and bruises. Rhythm, timing and Witch Hazel loves to bloom in the autumn and winter. She follows her own unique rhythm and that is her medicine." Horsetail smiled and Rose beamed. Witch Hazel sighed a beautiful sigh and said to Nimue, "This is your magic Nimue. Your gift."

Before long all of the plants wanted to share their medicine with Nimue. She remained in the forest learning all about them, their physical medicine and their spirit medicine. Her magic and talent grew so strong that her voice and the voice of the forest became one.

Nimue knew what her next step would be and jumped upon Cloud and asked him to take her to The Earth Keeper. Cloud glanced back at Nimue and shook his head in surprise while refusing to move. Nimue nudged him with her leg and Cloud remained at a standstill. He then leaned his head and neck to the earth, Nimue slid off at the bank of the river. She shook her little fist at Cloud and giggled, "You are so silly. Tell me what you know." Cloud neighed to her, "Just look at your reflection Nimue."

Nimue looked in the river and began to wash her face with the cold water. Cloud took a long drink. As Nimue splashed the cold water in her face she noticed a flicker of light in the river. She looked closer to get a better look. Staring back at her was a beautiful woman wearing a large silver pendant around her neck. She carried a large bow and had many pouches around her waist. The woman reached out for Nimue and spoke, "There are those that seek to control this world. Indeed to destroy all that is true because it is a threat to them. You have a light of power Nimue. Do not let anyone try to take that away. I know your strengths and your weaknesses. You do not know who you are. Only parts of yourself. Unconnected as yet. There is more for you to do. Go see Grandmother Hawthorn. She will teach you this. As will Elder. Go child and become yourself." She vanished in the water.

Nimue shouted to Cloud, "Did you see her, she was lovely but I am a bit frightened of her as well. Do you know why?" Cloud responded, "You know better than me Nimue."" Nimue snapped at Cloud, "I am tired of your riddles, just help me, tell me." Cloud turned away from Nimue and walked off with his head low. Nimue sat at the bank of river and began sobbing, "I am so sorry Cloud." Cloud turned and stepped towards her. He whinnied and pushed Nimue over. She began giggling and wrapped her small hands around his face and said, "I am sorry I shouted at you. Shadow woman scared me and I don't know who I am." Cloud gestured for Nimue to get on him and proceeded to their next destination.

CHAPTER 5

GRANDMOTHER HAWTHORN

Grandmother Hawthorn welcomed Nimue, "Ah, yes, Nimue I have been waiting for you." Nimue quietly replied, "Hello Grandmother Hawthorn. Grandmother Hawthorn asked Nimue, "What have you learned so far child?" Nimue answered, "I have learned what medicine is." Grandmother Hawthorn stared directly at Nimue and inquired, "Have you now? Hmmm so what is medicine?" Nimue said, 'Medicine is everywhere, in everything, in all parts of us. Our gifts that we bring to the world and the world of spirit." Grandmother Hawthorn then asked, "Now where does medicine come from?" Nimue remained silent. Grandmother Hawthorn smiled gently, "It comes from you Nimue. In order to use it you must travel to the darkest parts of yourself. Practicing medicine is not easy. It requires the courage to leave parts of yourself behind." Nimue spoke, "I don't think I have the courage to do that." Grandmother Hawthorn quietly said, "When all doubt disappears, that is when magic happens. Your medicine will only emerge from your uniqueness." Nimue questioned, "Like the Witch Hazel?" "Yes," answered Grandmother Hawthorn, "Like the Witch Hazel." "Ground yourself and allow your truth to emerge. Hold on to that voice." Nimue asked, "What if The Earth Keeper tries to take my power from me?" Grandmother Hawthorn nudged Nimue, "No one can take your power away unless you allow them to. Now follow the path deep into the Black Woods." There you will find The Elder." Nimue shook and said, "Grandmother Hawthorn I am afraid." "We are all one life my dear. You are not alone," replied Grandmother Hawthorn.

CHAPTER 6
THE EARTH KEEPER

Cloud and Nimue walked quietly through the wood. Cloud stopped in front of the Elder Tree. He bowed his head and Nimue dropped some tobacco at the base of the tree. The Elder Tree spoke, "Time and people are changing Nimue. The time has come to heal the earth. Nimue come closer. Touch my leaves and tell me what you feel." Nimue touched the leaves and said, "I feel medicine. The power of transformation." "You are ready," spoke The Elder Tree. Nimue started to get on Cloud. The Elder Tree stopped her, "NO Nimue. You must go alone. Nimue remember Rose, her medicine. Which part is more important her buds or her thorns?" Nimue grew silent and thought. She then said, "They are both important. You need all parts of yourself to be you. That is medicine." The Elder Tree smiled gently, "Now it is time for you to go. Place your hands firmly on the earth and wait for Mrs. Snake. She will show you the way. Follow her through the path under the earth to the Earth Keeper. You must go now." Nimue hesitated, "Will I be able to return." The Elder Tree answered, "That is up to you Nimue."

As the earth opened up beneath the Ancient Elder Tree Nimue fell into its moist darkness. She clutched at the roots as she spiraled down further and further, deeper and deeper. She landed with a thud, her body covered with dark green dust. She wondered what this magic could possibly mean. She found herself in a dark cavern deep beneath the earth. A voice from the shadows called out her name. Something about the voice made Nimue shudder with a burning pain in her heart. She could feel something inside herself dissolving. The voice in the shadows made a loud hissing sound and then began to sing. Nimue had to keep her mind on the task. She had to find and defeat The Earth Keeper. This was her only chance to restore the voices of the plants and the earth itself. She turned, wiped the dirt from her eyes and took a step forward into the dark.

A blue green mist appeared all around her making it difficult for her to see. Nimue began walking through the dark mist towards the sound of the voice. She noticed a large mirror in the distance with a lone figure standing beneath it. As Nimue came closer she saw an ancient woman dressed in black, her hunched back remained facing Nimue. All at once she stopped her singing. A stir of black wings filled the cavern. A burst of green light transforming the figure into the most beautiful woman Nimue had ever seen. The Earth Keeper turned facing Nimue, beautiful tall dark and vibrant, wearing an amulet of leaves and roots around her neck. Nimue was filled with terror and awe at this magical spirit. The spirit spoke out, "Who are you? What do you want? You seek to destroy me? And my world? You destroy me and you destroy yourself Nimue." Nimue questioned her, "What do you mean?" The Earth Keeper pointed to the mirror. Nimue was frozen in place but managed to walk towards the mirror. She saw herself and The Earth Keeper together. The Earth Keeper spoke the truth thought Nimue. The Earth Keeper spoke, "So you see we are the same." Nimue asked confused, "Are you my evil self? My bad self?' The Earth Keeper answered, "I am your dream self. The part of you that lives inside. Your true self." Nimue closed her eyes. She remembered what the plants had taught her. That she needed all parts of herself to be fully alive. Their eyes met. All this time Nimue believed she was supposed to destroy her, but she was wrong. She must free her. She took the amulet from around her neck and offered it to The Earth Keeper. The Earth Keeper said, "Come with me . I must show you something."

Deeper into the cave the two journeyed until they came upon a room of enchanted spiders weaving the most magnificent webs of light. Nimue gasped and exclaimed, "what are they doing?' The Earth Keeper answered, "They are weaving." Nimue questioned, "Do they ever stop?" The Earth Keeper replied, "Shhh look closely.' Nimue asked, "What are they weaving?" The Earth Keeper responded, "People's stories." Nimue noticed the patterns changing. The Earth Keeper continued, "The webs are people's dreams which become entwined with your dream self." Nimue watched as one by one the spiders fell from the web. Terrified Nimue asked The Earth Keeper, "What is happening to them?" The Earth Keeper replied sadly, "No one hears them anymore. On the outside they become twisted and distorted and the stories die forever. When people stop seeing beauty, they forget who they are. They forget their dreams and they lose their pure selves. Their spirits are lost. Then the plants are lost. Their voices will be heard no more and the world will forget and wither and die like people. I am the pattern and the spider. I am the pattern between dreams and spirit. I help things become." Nimue asked, "Become what?"

The Earth Keeper responded, "What they need to become. Your outward self your body is a face, a mask. Look deeper into the mirror. Beneath your outside there is the dream self." Nimue then said, "Yes, who I wish to be." The Earth Keeper told Nimue, "Look closer; hidden inside there is the core of your being. Who you are. How do stories become distorted? People are frightened of what they will find there. Other humans try to tell them what the truth is. Then they lose their caring. They lose their magic. And those that have magic are punished. People think I am different and strange. They believe I am evil. The people from my village talk about me. That is because they are afraid." Nimue questioned, "What are they afraid of?" The Earth Keeper pointed to the mirror, "The same thing you were afraid of Nimue."

Nimue looked at her reflection once again. She saw beyond her outside self and her dream self. She saw Nimue. She turned to embrace The Earth Keeper, but the Earth Keeper was gone.

CHAPTER 7
NIMUE RETURNS

The bus screeches to a halt as Nimue stumbles up the steps. The children laugh and yell at her, "The crippled witch can't even make it up the steps." Nimue grabs a window seat and waves to Cloud as the bus moves forward. Cloud winks back at Nimue. Nimue is smiling and holds the silver pendant at her neck. "Hey Witch kid," yells the little girl from the back of the bus, "you are nothing but weird." Nimue used her thorn side glaring back at her. Nimue smiled to herself again and remembered who she was. The truth would help her lead. The bus halted in front of the school. Nimue grabbed her backpack of herbs and started off the bus. As she walked up the path to the front doors, she heard the plants whispering, "Earth Keeper we are waiting for you to make it right." Nimue nodded at them as more and more plants began popping up at her feet. With each step a plant was growing. A crow flew overhead. Nimue had found herself.

Printed in the United States
By Bookmasters